The Road to Mumbai

by Ruth Jeyaveeran

Houghton Mifflin Company Boston 2004

In the middle of the night, Shoba's monkey, Fuzzy Patel, tickled her cheek.
Fuzzy was covered in fur except for the smooth spot on his tail that Shoba
used as a handle when she carried him.

"We must leave for Mumbai tonight," Fuzzy announced. "My dear cousin Poori is getting married there tomorrow."

"I love weddings!" Shoba said. She had flown to India once before on a jumbo jet with her parents.

"Ssshh," Fuzzy whispered. "This wedding is top-secret. It would be most improper if the common riffraff showed up, expecting to be invited."

Shoba knew that Fuzzy could be a bit of a snob, but before she could reply he unrolled a map of India. "While you were sleeping I was able to pinpoint our destination."

"Let's take the bed. Airplanes are so stuffy," Shoba said, sliding deep under the covers.

With a bump and a puff of smoke, the bed began to whir and spin, and they zoomed off into the night.

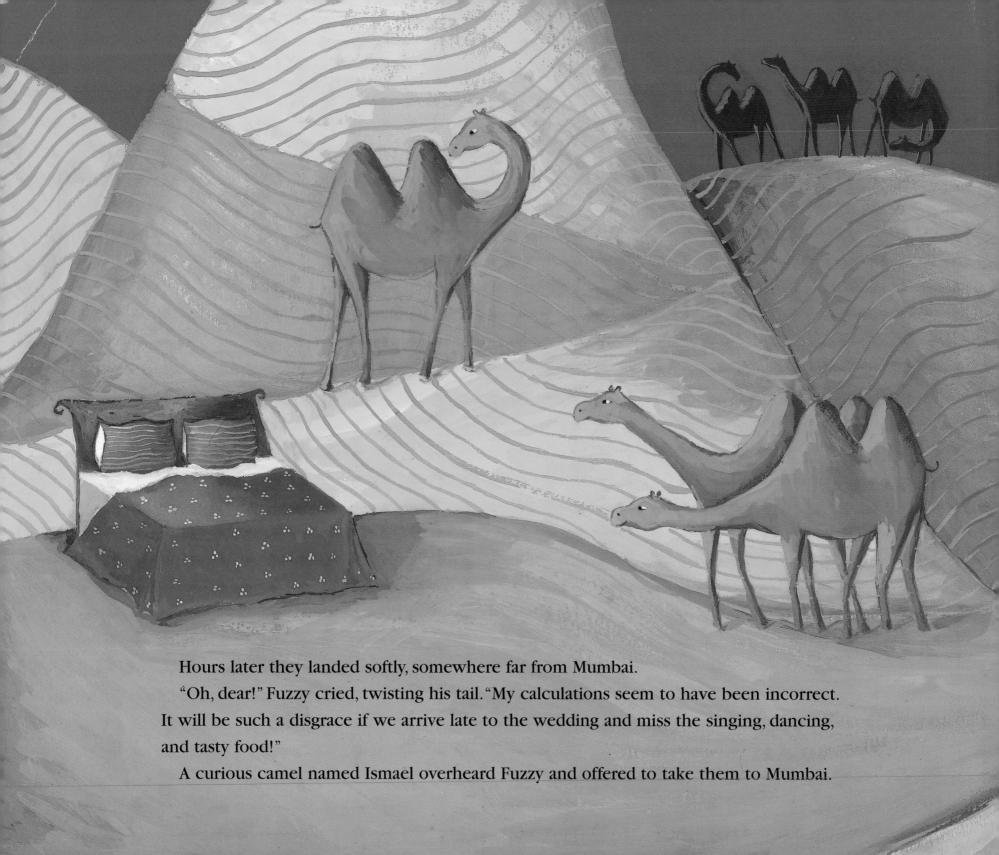

Hours later they landed softly, somewhere far from Mumbai.

"Oh, dear!" Fuzzy cried, twisting his tail. "My calculations seem to have been incorrect. It will be such a disgrace if we arrive late to the wedding and miss the singing, dancing, and tasty food!"

A curious camel named Ismael overheard Fuzzy and offered to take them to Mumbai.

As they trudged through the dry desert, Shoba grew hot and thirsty. Finally, they found the road to Mumbai and a boy named Anil, who was selling fresh coconut juice. When Shoba took a drink it felt like a cool waterfall running down to her toes.

As she sipped the last drops of juice, Shoba smiled. She had an idea. "Let's invite Ismael and Anil to the wedding."

"Oh, no, they would be bored to tears," Fuzzy said abruptly as he jumped down from Ismael's hump. "In fact, now that we're on the road to Mumbai, let's not trouble them any longer. Thank you, my dear camel, and farewell."

Before they continued on their journey, Shoba shook Anil's hand and gave Ismael a sandy kiss goodbye.

A few moments later they had to stop to let a line of elephants cross the road. Fuzzy twisted his tail impatiently. "This is most inconvenient."

"Excuse me, but we're late for a wedding," Shoba said politely to an elephant. Then she climbed up its trunk, ran across its back, and jumped down to the other side of the road.

"Wait for me!" Fuzzy cried. "And in case you were wondering," he called to the elephant, "this wedding will be quite dull—no singing, no dancing, and the portions of food will be far too small for an elephant to enjoy."

Around the corner Shoba saw a group of <u>monks</u> floating down the dirty street.

"Is this the way to Mumbai?" she asked one of them. "We're looking for a large wedding."

The monk didn't reply. "They've taken a vow of <u>silence</u>," Fuzzy whispered. Then he added loudly, "Surely these wise monks would prefer to spend their time in prayer, fasting, and <u>contemplation</u>, rather than to sing, dance, and eat tasty food at a monkey wedding. We shouldn't bother them with unimportant questions."

Farther down the road they found an old man sitting beside a large basket.

Suddenly the lid popped off.

Before Shoba could scream, the snake charmer pleaded, "Don't be afraid of Asha. Loud noises upset her digestion . . . Look!"
The snake and Fuzzy's tail had started to tango.

The old man joined in, playing a folk tune on the flute.

"How far is it to Mumbai?" Shoba asked. "We're going to a monkey wedding."

"What a joyous event!" the snake charmer cried, clapping his hands.

"Oh, no," Fuzzy assured him. "It will be a most unhappy event, especially for a snake with an artistic temperament and a sensitive stomach. I would never forgive myself if Asha's tail got trampled during the dancing."

"But Mumbai is in the other direction," the snake charmer told them. "Don't worry, though—the Mumbai Express should be arriving at any minute."

At that very moment the Mumbai Express rolled up to the corner. Running as fast as she could, Shoba grabbed Fuzzy, shut her eyes, and jumped.

It was getting dark when the bus finally reached Mumbai. Cars, scooters, bicycles, dogs, cows, rats, roosters, and rickshaws rumbled past them. The shiny saris of women walking beside the road fluttered like butterfly wings.

Fuzzy approached one of the women. "Pardon me, have you by chance seen a large striped tent?"

"There's one just down the road. Is it a wedding tent?" she asked eagerly.

"Yes, but it will be one of the most boring weddings in the history of the universe," he answered, scurrying past her.

In front of the tent Fuzzy's cousins Cecil, Kumar, and Raja were playing funky monkey music. Fuzzy looked around excitedly. "Where are all of the honored guests?"

"Well," said Kumar, "the Balrajes have a sick grandmonkey, the Tamarinds are expecting a little one, the Jaipurs are in Bali on vacation, the . . ."

"Oh, dear," Fuzzy interrupted as he twisted his tail. "This wedding
is going to be a disaster of enormous proportions."
    But before Fuzzy could twist his tail right off, Shoba cried, "Look!
I think the guests are arriving."

It was the best wedding Shoba and Fuzzy had ever been to. The air smelled of sweets and spices, and everyone ate laddoos, jelabees, and gulab jamun until the singing and dancing began. Then Poori and her new husband, Bikram, gave each guest a sparkling peacock feather before they hopped into a rickshaw to go on their honeymoon.

The next morning Shoba woke up with a start. On the pillow beside her Fuzzy snored softly, dreaming of the friends they had made on the road to Mumbai.

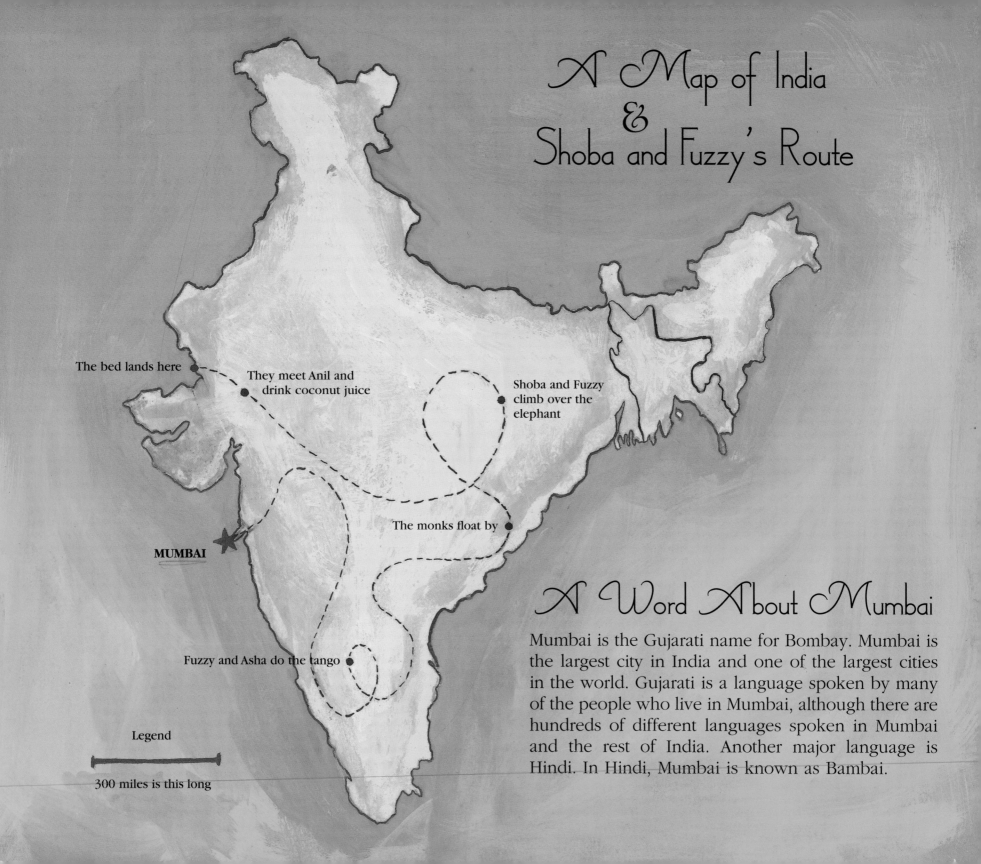

A Map of India
&
Shoba and Fuzzy's Route

The bed lands here

They meet Anil and
drink coconut juice

Shoba and Fuzzy
climb over the
elephant

The monks float by

MUMBAI

Fuzzy and Asha do the tango

Legend

300 miles is this long

A Word About Mumbai

Mumbai is the Gujarati name for Bombay. Mumbai is
the largest city in India and one of the largest cities
in the world. Gujarati is a language spoken by many
of the people who live in Mumbai, although there are
hundreds of different languages spoken in Mumbai
and the rest of India. Another major language is
Hindi. In Hindi, Mumbai is known as Bambai.

An Illustrated Glossary of Everyday Indian Things

fresh coconut juice clear, sweet juice from a young green coconut before it turns brown

gulab jamun round spongy balls made from milk that are fried and then covered in honey or rosewater syrup

jelabees pretzel-shaped sweets dipped in syrup

laddoos sweet round balls made of flour, butter, and sugar flavored with cardamom (an Indian spice), sometimes made with nuts and raisins

rickshaw a small carriage pulled by a person on foot or on a bicycle, usually used for short trips

sari the traditional dress worn by Indian women made from one long piece of cloth folded and draped around the body

© For my family ©

All rights reserved. For information about permission to reproduce
selections from this book, write to Permissions, Houghton Mifflin Company, 215
Park Avenue South, New York, New York 10003.

www.houghtonmifflinbooks.com

The text of this book is set in 14-point ITC Garamond 2.
The illustrations are gouache on illustration board.

ISBN-13: 978-0-618-43419-0
ISBN-10: 0-618-43419-4

Library of Congress Cataloging-in-Publication Data
Jeyaveeran, Ruth.
The road to Mumbai / by Ruth Jeyaveeran.
p. cm.
Summary: Shoba and her pet monkey, Fuzzy Patel, set out overnight by flying bed
to attend Fuzzy's cousin's wonderful wedding in Mumbai, India.
ISBN 0-618-43419-4
1. Weddings—Fiction. 2. Monkeys—Fiction. 3. Bombay (India) —Fiction. 4.
India—Fiction.
PZ7J565Ro 2004
[E]—dc22
2003019383

Printed in Singapore
TWP 10 9 8 7 6 5 4 3 2 1